CONTE

CHAPTER 1

EXTREME OBSTACLE

In the living room, twelve-year-old Tanisha Carter picked up the controller and settled onto the sofa. She was ready to play one of her favourite online multi-player games.

But before she could begin, her older brother, Terrell, walked into the living room. He dropped onto the sofa next to her.

"How long are you going to play your game for?" he asked. "There's a football game on in thirty minutes. I was hoping to watch it on the TV so I don't have to use my phone."

"That's just about enough time for me to play three levels of my game," Tanisha said. "The TV is all yours after that."

"Thanks!" said Terrell. "Have you seen

the new advert for *Rugged Reaper*? They're coming here next month. I know how much you love the TV programme."

Tanisha's eyes opened wide at the mention of her favourite show. "Wow!" she shouted. "Can you show it to me, NOW!"

Terrell chuckled as he loaded the advert onto his phone. "Calm down," he said, handing her the phone.

Tanisha could barely contain her excitement as she pressed play. Her mouth hung open as she watched children her own age barrel through an intense-looking obstacle course.

"This is fantastic!" she said.

"Do you think you know what an obstacle course is?" the announcer said.

Tanisha couldn't take her eyes off the screen. Exciting music played as the announcer's voice boomed.

"You've seen nothing until you've

challenged the Rugged Reaper," he continued. "The best obstacle course designed for children, by children!"

Tanisha watched *Rugged Reaper* every week. The competitors were fierce.

"This number-one show includes mud runs, balance beams, rope swings, wall climbing and the dreaded monkey bars of infinity!" the announcer continued. "And we're coming to a town near you!"

Tanisha paused the advert. "Are they really coming to Newville?" she asked her brother.

Terrell nodded. "I double-checked the website. We're one of their stops."

Tanisha pressed play again and listened to the rest of the details.

"The top three teams will advance to the national quarter-finals in Florida!" the announcer shouted.

"If you're between the ages of eight and

twelve and love to have fun, sign your two-person team up for this extreme obstacle course today!" the announcer finished.

Tanisha couldn't believe her luck. "I've always wanted to do this!" she said. "I'm going to get a teammate and sign up tomorrow!"

Terrell gave his younger sister a sceptical look. "Are you sure? It's one thing to watch it on TV. Do you really think you could cope with that type of challenge?" he said. "I don't think you'll be able to find a teammate and get ready that quickly. It's only a month away!"

"I can do anything I set my mind to," Tanisha snapped. "You'll see." She just had to find a teammate.

* * *

At school the next day, Tanisha sat with her friends in the canteen. She couldn't stop talking about *Rugged Reaper*.

"All I need is a teammate so we can sign

up and start training." Tanisha looked at her friend Justin. "Do you want to join my team?"

"I would," said Justin, taking a sip of his drink. "But it's football season. Practice and games take up most of my time."

Tanisha turned to her friend Nicole. "How about you?" she asked. "You're a great gymnast. We'd be unstoppable!"

Nicole made a face as she picked out the peas that had spilled into the dessert on her tray. "Sorry" she said. "My gymnastics coach won't let me take on any other extra-curricular activities."

Tanisha sighed. "It's OK," she said, even though she was disappointed. "I wouldn't want you to get into trouble."

She pushed her tray to one side and let out a sigh. *If none of my friends can do the Rugged Reaper with me, then what am I going to do?*

Just then Derek Reeves approached their

table. "Hi everyone, is it OK if I sit with you?" he asked, holding his tray of food.

"Yes, have a seat," Justin replied. "There's always room for one more."

"What's going on?" Derek asked, contemplating the mystery meat in his sandwich.

"Tanisha is trying to recruit a teammate so she can compete on *Rugged Reaper*," Nicole said. "Justin and I are both too busy, though."

"*Rugged Reaper*? Is it coming here? When?" Derek said, putting down his sandwich. "I'm obsessed with that programme. I watch it all the time. It looks like so much fun!"

Tanisha gave Derek a thoughtful look. "In May," she said. "My brother showed me the advert yesterday." She paused. "Would you like to be my teammate?"

Tanisha's friends seemed stunned.

"Can you imagine Derek on an obstacle

course?" Justin said. He shot the other boy a look. "No offence... It just doesn't seem like the type of thing you'd be interested in."

Unlike Justin, Derek wasn't in the football team and didn't seem to care about sports in general. He always seemed to struggle in PE, too. But he was one of the nicest people in the school.

"Because I'm a bit bigger? I might not be as athletic as you," Derek said, "but I'm strong."

"Derek did help us to win the tug-of-war against Mr Drexel's class," Nicole added.

"That's right! With your strength and my speed, we'll make an amazing team!" Tanisha exclaimed. "Not to mention how much we know about the TV programme. Will you do it? Will you be my teammate?"

"Of course!" Derek said, giving Tanisha a high five.

CHAPTER 2

IN TRAINING

Derek and Tanisha walked home together after school that day, planning out the next month before the big day.

"We need to start our training asap," Tanisha said.

"How will we train for it?" Derek asked. "It's not as though we can build a course, and the school playground isn't big enough."

"Well, we have to do something so we don't embarrass ourselves," Tanisha said.

Suddenly Derek stopped in his tracks and smiled. "Janet!" he exclaimed.

"Janet?" Tanisha repeated. She raised her eyebrow in confusion.

"My cousin Janet runs a gym," Derek

explained. "I don't know why I didn't think of it before."

"Do you think she'd let us train there?" Tanisha asked.

"It's worth a try. Let's drop in tomorrow after school and ask," he said.

"OK," Tanisha said, crossing her fingers. "Hopefully it'll work out. No pun intended!"

* * *

The next day after school, Tanisha and Derek went to Janet's gym, EveryFit. They opened the double doors to the gym, looking on in awe.

"This gym is huge!" Tanisha exclaimed.

Janet left her office and walked over to Derek and Tanisha. "Hi, Derek," she said, giving him a hug. "Your mum told me you might be popping in."

"Hi, Janet," Derek replied. "This is my

friend Tanisha from school. We're signing up to compete on *Rugged Reaper* next month and need somewhere to train. Any chance we can train here?"

Janet thought for a moment. "I don't see why not," she said.

"Fantastic!" Tanisha and Derek shouted, high-fiving each other.

Janet held up a hand. "Two conditions, though," she said. "First, you help at the gym for a couple of hours a week. Second, you let me train you."

Derek and Tanisha looked at each other and turned to Janet. "Deal!" they said in unison.

"Where do we start?" Derek asked. "How about the climbing wall over there? I know there's one in the Rugged Reaper course. That would help us prepare."

Tanisha felt uneasy looking at the massive

climbing wall. It was more than seven metres high. She was overwhelmed by its height.

"Perhaps we shouldn't start with anything too hard today," she said. She pointed at the rowing machines. "Those look interesting."

Janet shook her head. "You're doing an obstacle course with a lot of running and endurance activities," she said. "Let's start with cardio and circuit training. Go to the changing rooms and change into your gym kit, then meet me in the training area."

Tanisha and Derek did as they were told. Minutes later, they were standing with Janet at one of the training areas.

"All right, let's warm up and stretch a bit before we start," Janet said. "Warming up and stretching improves your heart rate and prevents fatigue. It also minimizes your risk of pulling or straining a muscle."

Janet showed Tanisha and Derek how to

properly stretch their calves, hips, arms, necks, legs and shoulders. Then they were ready to begin.

"Let's start a circuit of twenty push-ups, sit-ups and jumping jacks," Janet said. "Go!"

Derek and Tanisha had no problem doing the push-ups. But as Tanisha blazed through her sit-ups and began her jumping jacks, Derek struggled.

When she'd finished her jumping jacks, Tanisha looked at Derek. "Come on, Derek, you can do it," she said. "Only four more to go!"

Derek completed his sit-ups and quickly did his jumping jacks. By the time he'd finished, he was breathing heavily.

"Sorry, T," Derek said, panting. "I don't want to slow us down. I've never been good at sit-ups."

"It's OK. It's our first day. The more we

train, the better we'll get!" Tanisha said, trying to sound positive. "We just have to support each other."

"She's right," Janet agreed, nodding. "Having a supportive partner makes a big difference. But so does training, so let's get back to work! Another round of push-ups, sit-ups and jumping jacks. Let's go!"

When they'd completed a few sets, Janet led them over to the balance beam. It looked just like the one on *Rugged Reaper.*

"You'll need to do some balance training," Janet said. "Climb up onto the beam and slowly walk across it. Focus on your centre of gravity and posture. The more you practise, the quicker you'll be able to do it."

Derek got onto the beam first. After only few steps, he lost his balance and fell off the beam. He landed on the mat below with a *thud*!

"Oof!" Derek coughed.

Tanisha stepped onto the beam next. She was halfway across and feeling good, so she decided to speed up a bit. Almost immediately she lost her balance and fell on the mat.

"Ow," she muttered. "This gym needs softer mats."

"What did I say before you got on the beam?" Janet asked.

"Slowly walk across the beam, and the more we practise, the better we'll get," Tanisha said.

Janet nodded. "That's right. Now both of you get back on the beam and try again."

CHAPTER 3

A TALL PROBLEM

Tanisha and Derek continued training with Janet at the gym every day after school. That weekend, they helped at the gym as repayment. After a week of training, they were already starting to see some improvement.

"I can actually run a couple of laps around the track without getting tired or taking a break," Derek said. "I've never been able to do that before!"

"I know!" Tanisha agreed. "And your cousin's nutrition tips have been a big help. I've been drinking more water and not eating as much junk food. I don't feel as sluggish as I did last week."

"We're going to be great on *Rugged Reaper*!" Derek said.

"I can't wait!" Tanisha agreed.

Janet approached them. "Looks like you two are ready for training today," she said.

"Definitely," Tanisha agreed. "And we got an e-mail with additional rules about the course. You can help your partner on the terror wall and infinity monkey bars."

"But if one of the players falls off an obstacle, he or she has to start the obstacle all over again," Derek added.

Janet walked them over to the gym's climbing wall. "Speaking of walls, I think today is the right time for both of you to do some climbing."

Tanisha and Derek looked up at the climbing wall in front of them. It stretched all the way to the ceiling.

"Ooh," Tanisha said. The wall seemed even higher than she remembered.

Janet helped both Tanisha and Derek into their climbing harnesses. Then she secured their bungee ropes.

"When climbing, remember that your legs are stronger than your arms," she told them. "So focus on your foot and leg placement. And take your time today. This is new for both of you."

Derek approached the wall first. "I can do this," he said under his breath.

Tanisha watched as Derek started to climb. She froze where she stood as she realized how tall the wall was.

"Tanisha, are you going to start climbing?" Janet asked.

Tanisha gulped nervously. "Um, yes," she said. "I was just watching how well Derek is doing. I'll make a start."

Derek was already near the top of the wall as Tanisha began.

"I can do this. I can do this," Tanisha repeated to herself. She placed her foot on the first foothold.

As Tanisha neared the halfway mark on the wall, she paused. Looking up, she saw Derek start to make his descent back down. Then she looked down. Janet looked like a tiny speck down below.

Tanisha started to sweat. Her fingers tingled. She'd never been up this high before.

"Are you OK?" Derek asked, pausing near her. He looked concerned.

Tanisha sweated even more. "Um, I'm not feeling very well all of a sudden. I'm sorry."

"It's all right," Derek said. "Do you want me to help you down?"

"No, no, it's OK," she said. "Just give me a few minutes. I'll get down."

Tanisha wheezed. Only halfway up the wall, and she felt as if she couldn't breathe, let alone move. If she looked up, the wall seemed even more terrifying. If she looked down, she felt as though she was going to be sick.

She'd never felt like this before, but it suddenly hit her – she was scared of heights. And if she couldn't conquer her fear, she'd embarrass herself on television – and let her teammate down.

CHAPTER 4

FEAR

Later that week, Tanisha was sitting at the kitchen table, doing her homework, when Terrell walked in.

"Hello," he said. He went straight to the fridge to get a drink. "*Rugged Reaper* is on. Do you want to watch it?"

"No thanks," Tanisha said, looking through her textbook.

"But you never miss an episode," Terrell replied. "I'm sure Mum and Dad won't mind if you finish–"

"I said I don't want to watch it!" Tanisha snapped.

Terrell looked shocked. "OK! What's the matter?" he said.

"Nothing," Tanisha said, shaking her head.

Terrell pushed Tanisha's textbook away and sat next to her at the table. "Come on, tell me what's wrong?"

Tanisha sighed. "Derek and I were training earlier this week, and I froze on the climbing wall. It seems as though I'm scared of heights. Now I don't know if I can do this. Perhaps you were right. Perhaps I can't do the Rugged Reaper after all."

Terrell shook his head. "I was just trying to be funny. You and Derek have been working too hard on this for you to give up."

"But what if I mess it up? I'll be letting Derek down, too," Tanisha replied.

"You'll never know unless you try. And I believe in you. You should talk to Janet or Derek about this. I'm sure they'll be able to help," Terrell said.

* * *

Tanisha got to her next training session early, hoping to tackle her fear. She put on her climbing harnesses and secured her bungee rope. Looking up at the wall, she began to climb.

But after only three small levels, Tanisha's heart began to pound. She looked up at the top of the wall and began to sweat heavily. She was too scared to climb any higher.

Tanisha quickly got down from the wall, removing the bungee rope and harness.

What am I going to do? she worried.

A moment later, Derek walked up. "Hello!" he called. "I got here early to do some pull-ups before we started training. I can do twenty in a row before I get tired!" To prove his point, he picked Tanisha up off the ground.

"OK, OK!" Tanisha laughed as Derek put her back down.

Just then, Janet walked over. She got them going straight away on a set of push-ups.

"Well done!" Janet said as they finished. "You're both blazing through those!"

"I'm still too slow with my sit-ups, though," Derek complained.

"But you're really good at jumping jacks," Tanisha reminded him. "And you've improved on the balance beam this week."

"You're both doing well," Janet agreed. "I think it's time to make it a bit harder." She put ankle weights on both Derek and Tanisha.

"What are these for?" Derek asked. "Isn't running already hard enough?"

"It's going to be even harder in the mud," Janet replied. "These will help prepare you."

Derek started running around the gym. "They feel strange–" He suddenly lost his balance and fell to the floor.

Tanisha ran towards Derek. "Are you all right–" she began. But then she fell over too, landing on top of Derek. They both laughed.

Janet helped them back to their feet. "They'll also help you with your balance," she told them with a laugh. "Now, I want both of you to walk around the track a few times. Don't run. I don't want you hurting yourselves."

Derek and Tanisha began to walk around the track. "Tanisha?" Derek said as they started their first lap.

"Yes," Tanisha replied.

"I just wanted to say thanks for asking me to be your teammate," Derek said. "I know I wasn't your first choice. And I'm not the most athletic. But you've been a great friend through all of this. I'm really looking forward to the competition."

"You're welcome," said Tanisha. "This has been a lot of fun for me, too."

But memories of being stuck on the wall – too scared to climb – began to creep in again.

"Can I tell you something?" she asked.

"Of course," Derek nodded. "What is it?"

Tanisha opened her mouth to tell Derek about her fear, but something stopped her. She shouldn't be scared. Not of something as silly as heights.

She was the athlete on the team. If Derek, who'd had to work harder, was doing so well, she couldn't let her friend and teammate down. The last thing she wanted was for him to have to worry about her, too.

Derek has his own stuff to worry about, Tanisha thought. *I'm going to have to conquer my fear on my own.*

"Oh actually, it's nothing," she said. "I'll tell you another time. Shall we see if Janet will let us do monkey-bar training and tummy-crawl drills after our laps?"

CHAPTER 5

HIDING SOMETHING

After weeks of training, it was time for Derek and Tanisha's final session at the gym.

"So, what's the plan today?" Derek asked Janet.

"How about some push-ups and sit-ups, followed by some crawling drills?" asked Tanisha.

Janet handed them each a package. "Not today. You have trained enough. You're ready. Here's a present for each of you for all of your hard work."

"Wow, thanks!" Derek said as they opened their presents. Inside each was a red T-shirt and matching shorts that said *EveryFit Champions*.

"Now you'll be the best-looking team in the competition," Janet said, smiling. "Your event is in two days time, so I want both of you to eat well – no junk food. Drink lots of water, stay away from distractions and computer games, and get a good night's sleep."

"Will do," Tanisha promised.

"I told both of your parents that tonight would be short, so they're waiting for you outside. Good luck. No matter what happens, I'm proud of you both."

Derek gave Janet a big hug. "I really appreciate that," he said. Turning to Tanisha, he added, "I'll see you at school tomorrow!"

"See you!" said Tanisha. After Derek had left, she sighed, lowering her head.

"What's wrong?" Janet asked.

Tanisha tried to brush it off. "Nothing. Why?"

"I can see it on your face," Janet replied. "What's worrying you?"

Tanisha let out a big sigh. "It's … the climbing wall. I-I-I'm scared of heights," she managed to get out. "I didn't realize it before we started training, but the wall is so tall, and it really scares me. It'll be my fault if we lose *Rugged Reaper.*"

"Why didn't you say something about this sooner?" Janet asked, looking concerned.

Embarrassed, Tanisha looked down at her feet. "I don't know. It's just … I didn't want to admit I was scared," she said. "I didn't want to let Derek down. I'm supposed to be the athlete."

"You're *supposed* to be a team," Janet replied.

"I know," Tanisha said. "And now when we reach the wall I'm going to panic and not be able to do it."

Janet put her arm around Tanisha's shoulders. "You know, it's OK to be scared, Tanisha," she said. "We all get scared about certain things. When I was your age, I was terrified of the water."

"Water?" Tanisha repeated. She was confused. "Why?"

"I thought I would drown," Janet replied. "I wouldn't go near a swimming pool or beach for a long time. It wasn't until I decided to face my fear that I was able to overcome it. I didn't do it alone. But I did it. And you can, too."

Tanisha nodded sceptically. She wanted to believe Janet, but...

"Is it OK if I tell my mum to wait for a bit? Do you have time to help me on the climbing wall?" she asked.

"Of course," said Janet. "We'll get through it together."

Tanisha went to tell her mum she needed a bit more time. When she came back, Janet was at the climbing wall putting on her equipment. Tanisha got into her harness, too.

"When we start climbing I want you to focus on your hands, feet and the wall in front of you," Janet said. "Focus on these three things and don't look up."

"But what if I get–" Tanisha started to say.

Janet read her mind. "If you get scared, close your eyes, take a deep breath, exhale and calm yourself. Then continue to move up the wall and focus on the three things," she said.

Tanisha nodded and took a deep breath. She began to climb slowly, with Janet climbing right next to her. At first it was slow going, but about halfway up the wall, Tanisha began to move a little bit faster.

"You're doing so well!" Janet shouted.

Tanisha smiled as she looked at Janet. But then she looked up. Her fear of heights came racing back.

"I'm here next to you, Tanisha," Janet said. "Don't panic. Remember what I told you to do if you get scared."

Tanisha stopped looking up, looked at Janet and then closed her eyes. She took a deep breath, exhaled and looked directly at the wall. She began climbing again.

Tanisha and Janet finished climbing the wall, then made their way back down.

When they reached the bottom, Tanisha gave Janet a big hug.

"It was scary, but I did it," Tanisha said. "Will you climb the wall with me again?"

"I'd be happy to," Janet replied.

CHAPTER 6

THE RUGGED REAPER

The big day had finally arrived. Derek and Tanisha met up at the Newville Fields Park early in the morning. Before long, the stands had filled up with *Rugged Reaper* fans, along with the families and friends of the contestants.

Derek and Tanisha took their places at the starting line. The rest of the contestants lined up as well.

"Can you believe the turnout? There must be hundreds of us waiting to do this course!" said an excited Derek.

"I had no idea it would be *this* big," Tanisha said. "Look at all the TV cameras. This is wild!"

Just then a couple of contestants walked up to Tanisha and Derek. "Hi, I'm Blake," one of the boys said. "This is my friend, Austin."

"I'm Derek, and this is Tanisha," Derek replied. "Nice to meet you both!"

"Is this your first extreme obstacle course?" Blake asked.

Tanisha nodded. "How about you?"

"This is our third," Austin replied. "When we found out that *Rugged Reaper* was coming here, we had to come and have a go."

"Is there any advice you can give us?" Derek asked.

"Accept that you're going to get very muddy almost immediately!" joked Blake.

"And never leave your teammate behind," Austin added.

Just then the announcer made her way to the podium. "Greetings, and welcome to *Rugged Reaper*! Are you all ready?"

Everyone screamed, "Yes!" in unison.

"Good! Now, because the top three teams will advance to the national quarter-finals, we've made this course especially challenging. There's a special, never-before-seen final obstacle!" the announcer bellowed. "When the pistol fires, begin! Good luck!"

The starter pistol blared, and the contestants ran to the first obstacle, the massive mud run. Tanisha and Derek sped off through the mud, dodging the splashes the other children were making as they ran.

A few people fell face-first into the mud, causing a chain reaction. Even some of the cameramen got caught up in it. Staying upright, Derek overtook them, followed by Tanisha.

"Janet was clever to make us use those ankle weights!" Tanisha shouted.

"Definitely!" Derek shouted back. "We're almost out of the mud!"

The two finished the mud run and ran quickly to the second obstacle, the baited tummy crawl. It was a forty-metre ground crawl under a net.

Tanisha and Derek wiggled under the net and started crawling. Just in front of them, some children got tangled in the net, slowing them down.

Manoeuvring past them, Tanisha crawled quickly on the ground like a mini-locomotive. Derek trailed behind her.

"The net ahead is hanging low, so don't get tangled, Derek!" Tanisha warned.

"Thanks, partner!" Derek said.

After what seemed like an eternity, Derek and Tanisha finished the crawl. They ran with the others to the third obstacle, the sit-up situation station. Adults had been stationed there to make sure everyone did fifty sit-ups.

Tanisha and Derek arrived at their station and began their repetitions. Tanisha flew through her fifty sit-ups. When she had finished, Derek still had twenty-five more to do.

Tanisha got up and cheered her teammate on. "Come on, Derek! You can do it!"

Tanisha was really impressed with how far Derek had come. He finished his sit-ups, and they began running again.

"We've got a 500-metre run now, up to our next station," Tanisha said. "Let's go!"

CHAPTER 7

BALANCE, SWING AND HOLD ON!

Nearing the completion of the run, Tanisha and Derek were in second place. They were making good time on the course so far.

Around the bend was a volunteer water station to make sure the contestants stayed hydrated. As they ran towards the station, Tanisha saw a familiar face standing there, holding cups of water.

"Terrell?" she exclaimed. "What are you doing here?"

"Trying to be supportive," her brother said, handing her a cup. "Now, don't get distracted by me. Go, go, go!"

Derek and Tanisha both gulped some water and kept running. Soon they arrived at the next obstacle station, the stability beam and swing. It had sets of extended balance beams and a rope swing at the end. A pool of water had been set up underneath the whole obstacle.

"The first-place team is only halfway across the beams. We can catch up with them!" said Derek.

Tanisha began to make her way slowly along the balance beam. Behind her, the other teams were starting to catch up and test their skills on the beam. Most went too fast and fell in the water, meaning they had to start again at the beginning of the beam.

Tanisha was almost at the end of the balance beam. She grabbed the rope to swing towards dry land when she heard ... *SPLASH!*

Derek had fallen into the water just before reaching the end of the balance beam. He now had to go back to the beginning of the beam and start all over again.

"Oh no!" Tanisha cried out after landing on the ground. The teams behind her raced to the next station, pushing Tanisha and Derek out of second place.

"I'm so sorry!" Derek shouted. He crossed the beam again, making it to the end this time and grabbing the rope. He swung to dry land and landed next to Tanisha. "I've messed up everything!"

"No, you haven't. Stop beating yourself up and let's get moving!" Tanisha shouted as they raced to the next station, the push-ups of doom.

Each team member had to do one hundred push-ups before being allowed to move forward. Most of the teams were struggling. Everyone was exhausted.

Tanisha grinned. This was the perfect opportunity to catch up.

An adult watched as they each did one hundred push-ups and were cleared to go to the next station. Their training was paying off!

"We're not too far from the fourth-place team. We still have a chance!" Tanisha said as she and Derek ran down the trail.

"Get ready for the infinity monkey bars!" Derek warned.

Derek started the monkey bars first. Tanisha was just behind him. Halfway through, she started to tire. She tried desperately to hold on.

Like the balance beams, if a contestant fell before completing the bars, he or she had to start all over again. Instead of a pool of water below, however, it was a pond of mud.

"All those push-ups wore my arms out," Tanisha said, panting. "I'm having trouble holding on–"

Suddenly she lost her grip. Tanisha fell, waiting to hear the splash of the mud before her. Instead, she was hanging in mid-air.

Derek was clinging to the monkey bars with one hand. He'd used his other hand to save Tanisha from falling!

"You didn't give up on me when I fell, and I'm not giving up on you!" Derek said.

One of the cameramen moved closer to Derek and Tanisha, capturing the moment. Derek rocked Tanisha back and forth until she could reach the monkey bars. Together, they finished making their way across.

On the sidelines, a judge said, "Teammates can prevent their partner from falling, so she has the all clear to continue!"

Derek and Tanisha smiled. Then Derek said, "Take a quick breather, and then let's get going!"

CHAPTER 8

THE WALL

Derek and Tanisha ran up the trail to the next obstacle, the rock-with-you wall.

Tanisha was shocked to see a very short version of the wall she and Derek had climbed at EveryFit during their training sessions.

"That's it?" she cried. "That's the wall? That's a breeze! We'll catch up with the third-place team in no time!"

Together, Derek and Tanisha quickly scaled the wall. They jumped off onto a massive, cushioned landing pad.

"I can see the third-place team, they're not too far ahead!" Derek shouted. "We can catch up with them on the trail!"

They started running down the trail, and soon they were within reach of the third-place team. But then they went around the bend to the final obstacle. All the teams paused and stood in awe of the mother wall, a 12-metre-tall, forward-leaning wall.

Tanisha gulped. She stood there, frozen with fear, as the other teams grabbed ropes and started pulling themselves up the wall.

Derek grabbed a rope too and was about to climb when he realized that Tanisha hadn't moved. "Are you OK?" he called.

"I can't do it, Derek!" Tanisha screamed to her partner. "I'm scared of heights. That wall is just too tall!"

"I'm scared of this wall, too!" Derek shouted back.

"What are you talking about? You had no problem climbing that big wall at the gym!" Tanisha said.

"Only because I was trying to hurry up and get it over with," Derek explained. "I've been intimidated by it throughout our training. But we've worked hard to get here, and we still have a chance to get third place. The other teams are struggling! Win or lose, we do it together."

Tanisha shook her head and stared up at the wall. It loomed high above her. But then she remembered what Janet had taught her in the gym.

"You're right," Tanisha finally replied. "I might be scared, but we can do this!"

Derek and Tanisha both grabbed a rope and began making their way up the wall. Tanisha's nerves were getting the better of her, but she tried to focus on the wall, her hands and her feet as she climbed up. Derek cheered her on as they climbed.

"I'm here with you!" he called.

Finally they both made it to the top of the wall and looked back down at the wall behind them. They'd come a long way. On the other side, the third-place team had just landed.

Tanisha and Derek nodded at each other, then held each other's hand as they climbed over the top and jumped down. They landed, screaming, onto the pad below.

"We've done it!" Tanisha cheered. "I can't believe it!"

"It's not over yet! We've still got half a kilometre to run," Derek said. "Let's catch up with the other teams and win this!"

CHAPTER 9

THE FINAL STRETCH

Tanisha and Derek continued down the trail, getting closer and closer to the third-place team. They were both still holding out hope that they would qualify for the finals on *Rugged Reaper*.

"This run seems like it's taking forever!" said Tanisha.

The first- and second-place teams were so far ahead that Derek and Tanisha couldn't see them. But as they approached the dip in the trail, the third-place team tripped!

"We can pass them!" said Derek.

The third-place team quickly got up off the ground. But Tanisha and Derek were right next to them!

There were cameras everywhere. Tanisha could see loads more of them at the finish line up ahead.

"Look! There's the finish line!" Tanisha shouted as they ran side-by-side. "We can do this!"

The final sprint felt like a lifetime. All four children ran as fast as they could towards the finish! Tanisha's heart was racing as she breathed heavily. Next to her, Derek was panting for air.

"We're almost there!" said Tanisha.

With a sudden flash, they crossed the finish line! They'd done it! They'd completed the Rugged Reaper!

"How have we done? Have we got third place?" Tanisha asked.

"I don't know," said Derek, gasping for breath. "It was so close. We were right next to them as we crossed the line."

Together they stood on the sidelines, waiting to hear who would take third place.

"You two are really good," said one of the children on the other team. "How many of these obstacle courses have you done before?"

"This is our first," replied Tanisha.

"Really? It doesn't seem like it!"

Just then, the announcer's voice came over the loudspeaker. "That was a photo finish for third place! Are you ready to hear who made it to the finals?"

The crowd cheered, and Derek grabbed Tanisha's hand.

"Good luck," Tanisha said, crossing her fingers.

"All four of our contestants did brilliantly," the announcer continued, "but today, Tony and Billie crossed the line first. They advance to the finals!"

Next to Derek and Tanisha, the other team cheered. Disappointed, Tanisha and Derek shook their hands.

"Congratulations," Derek said.

"Thanks!" the other team said. "Hope to see you at another event!" They walked away to collect their third-place medals.

Tanisha was upset. "I'm sorry, Derek. My fear of heights at the mother wall put us behind. That's why we lost."

"That's not true," Derek said. "I fell on the balance beam. We both made mistakes. But together we beat our fears and did something a lot of first-timers could never do! We came this close to going to the finals! How brilliant is that?"

"You're right!" Tanisha said, smiling. "We should be proud of ourselves!"

Derek gave Tanisha a hug. "You're a great teammate and friend," he said.

"You too," said Tanisha.

A moment later, Derek and Tanisha's friends and families came over. Everyone was eager to congratulate them.

"I can't believe how well you two did!" said Terrell.

"Not bad for a girl, huh?" Tanisha joked. She looked to Janet. "Is it OK if I come over on Monday to train?"

"Me too!" said Derek. "We're a team!"

"But the event is over," Janet said. "You completed the course."

"We want to start getting ready for next year!" said Tanisha.

"Yes!" cheered Derek, fist-bumping Tanisha. "Let's do it!"

AUTHOR BIO

Shawn Pryor is the creator and co-writer of the all-ages graphic novel mystery series Cash & Carrie, writer of *Kentucky Kaiju* and writer and co-creator of the 2019 GLYPH-nominated football/drama series Force. He is also the author of the Jake Maddox Sports Stories title *Diamond Double Play*. In his spare time, Shawn enjoys reading, cooking, listening to music and talking about why Zack from the *Mighty Morphin Power Rangers* is the greatest superhero of all time.

ILLUSTRATOR BIO

After graduating from the Institute for Cinema and Television in Rome, in 1995, Giuliano Aloisi began working as an animator, layout artist and storyboard artist on TV series and TV games for RAI TV. He went on to illustrate for the comic magazine *Lupo Alberto* and for *Cuore*, a satirical weekly magazine. Giuliano continues to work as an animator and illustrator for advertising companies and educational publishing

GLOSSARY

centre of gravity point at which the entire weight of something can be balanced

circuit training workout technique involving a series of exercises performed in a rotation with minimal rest, often using different pieces of equipment

competitor person who tries to win a race or contest

descent moving from a higher to a lower place

endurance ability to keep doing an activity for long periods of time

fatigue great tiredness

hydrated having achieved a healthy balance of fluids in the body

massive very large, heavy and solid

nutrition study of how bodies use food to stay strong and healthy

obstacle object that you have to go around or over; something that blocks your path

overwhelmed completely overcome by thoughts or feelings

posture position of your body

sceptical doubt that something is true

sluggish slow in movement or reaction

unison in exact agreement or at the same time

DISCUSSION QUESTIONS

1. Imagine that *Rugged Reaper* is coming to your local town and you are selected to compete. Who would you choose to be your partner and why? Discuss which qualities would make the person a good teammate for the obstacle course.

2. Tanisha and Derek spent weeks training and exercising in order to prepare for the extreme obstacle course. What kind of exercises would you do to prepare for an obstacle course?

3. Tanisha doesn't want to share her fear of heights with Derek because she doesn't want to let him down. Do you think that was a fair reaction? Discuss other ways that Tanisha could have handled the situation.

WRITING PROMPTS

1. Imagine you've been given the task of creating an obstacle course for your classmates and friends. What kind of obstacles would you include on your course? Draw a map and write a few paragraphs explaining your obstacles and the course.

2. It can be interesting to think about a story from a different point of view. Try writing Chapter 7 from Derek's point of view. What do you think was going through his mind when he fell off the balance beam and into the water?

3. Tanisha discovers that she has a fear of heights when she starts training. Have you ever had a fear of heights or a different fear that you conquered? Write two or three paragraphs about what your fear was and how you overcame it.

MORE ABOUT
EXTREME OBSTACLE COURSES

Extreme obstacle courses have grown popular in recent years. In 2017, more than six million people signed up to participate in obstacle courses worldwide. Obstacle course running has become so popular that colleges and universities have even launched organizations and teams that feature obstacle course training.

One of the toughest obstacle courses of all time is the World's Toughest Mudder. Unlike other obstacle courses, this course runs for twenty-four hours! The course can be as short as 8 kilometres or as long as 20 kilometres. But all contestants must loop the course continuously until the clock runs out.

In order to qualify for the World's Toughest Mudder, a contestant must first be one of the finalists in a Tough Mudder race. All obstacles for the Tough Mudder are kept secret until the day of the event. That way no one knows what they're preparing for – the whole course is a surprise for everyone who runs it.

On average, only ten per cent (or fewer) of the World's Toughest Mudder contestants actually complete the challenge.

ONE OF THE EARLIEST OBSTACLE COURSES IN HISTORY

One of the earliest obstacle-based competitions happened during the 1900 Summer Olympic Games in Paris, during the two-hundred-metre obstacle swim.

This wasn't a typical swimming event – it featured three types of obstacles that swimmers had to face in the water:

1. A pole that every swimmer had to climb over

2. A group of rowing boats that swimmers had to climb over

3. A group of rowing boats that swimmers had to swim under

The event was held over a span of two days, with Frederick Lane of Austria winning the gold medal.

THE FUN DOESN'T STOP HERE!

You can find more of your favourite characters and exciting Sport Stories at:

www.raintree.co.uk